THE ESSENTIAL GUIDE

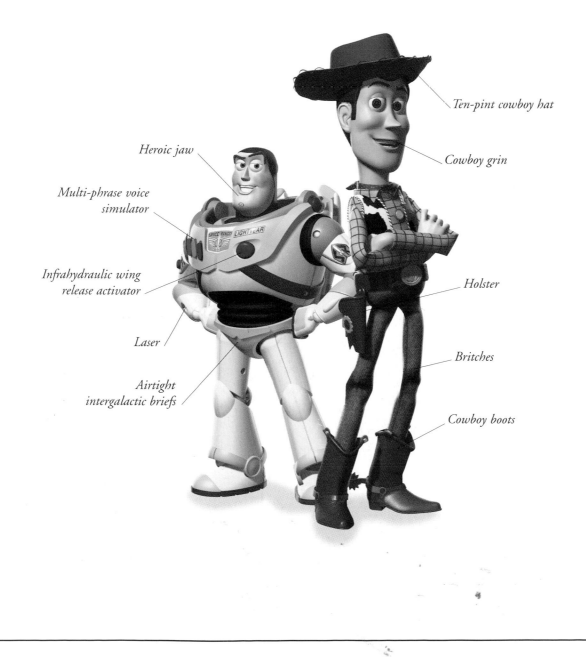

Ten-pint cowboy hat

Cowboy grin

Heroic jaw

Multi-phrase voice simulator

Infrahydraulic wing release activator

Holster

Laser

Britches

Airtight intergalactic briefs

Cowboy boots

HAMM

Pink plastic exterior

Trifocal eyes

ALIEN

Zurgotronic ion blaster

EVIL EMPEROR ZURG

Detachable parts

MR. POTATO HEAD

Roundup Ranch belt buckle

JESSIE

Fake cowhide chaps

Floppy prospector's hat

Mining pick

PROSPECTOR

Disney · PIXAR

TOY STORY

THE ESSENTIAL GUIDE

Itty bitty eyes

REX

Toothy grin

Tiny arms

Zurg whacker

Dorling Kindersley Publishing, Inc.

CONTENTS

ZURG

WOODY

REX

BO PEEP

MR. POTATO HEAD

MRS. POTATO HEAD

ALIEN

BUZZ

HOWDY!

Welcome to the world of *Toy Story*. A magical place
where, once the humans leave and the doors close, the
toys come out to play! Find out how they live together,
cope with new arrivals, and explore the sometimes
dangerous, but always exciting, outside world. See the
latest additions to a space ranger's uniform, tremble at
the evil Emperor Zurg—the most powerful toy in the
universe—and be slightly impressed by Hamm's wisdom.
Now turn the page, and let the Essential Guide take you
on a journey where your toys come to life!

BULLSEYE

JESSIE

PROSPECTOR

HAMM

SLINKY

"Howdy!"

Woody

Meet the leader of the gang. A pull-string doll from the 1950s, Woody is Andy's favorite toy. But this is threatened by the new toy on the block—Buzz Lightyear. The adventures these two go through lead to some amazing discoveries, including a past that Woody never knew he had.

Hand-stitched polyvinyl hat

Heroic western jaw

Bandanna

Shiny gold sheriff's badge

Fake cowhide vest

Cotton shirt

Roundup Ranch belt buckle

Holster

Britches

Spurs

Boot straps

Cowboy boots

Toy Microphone

Woody takes charge at all of the toy meetings. Using the amplifying power of Mr. Mike, Woody is able to speak above the noise of the others, including the know-it-all comments of Hamm and Mr. Potato Head.

WOODY PROFILE

• Woody was the star of his own TV series from the 1950s—*Woody's Roundup*. Other stars of the series include Bullseye the horse, Jessie the yodelling cowgirl, and Stinky Pete the Prospector.

• The show was finally taken off the air when kids started to play with space toys, leaving Woody suspended over the Grand Canyon in the last episode—the ultimate cliff-hanger!

• Woody lists his hobbies as ropin' and havin' fun. His favorite sayings include "Somebody's Poisoned the Water Hole."

Taking Charge

Even outside the paradise of Andy's room, Woody's leadership skills shine through. Under his guidance and after resourceful planning, the mutant toys rescue Buzz from the clutches of Sid, giving Buzz and Woody the chance to return to Andy.

To hear Woody speak, all Andy has to do is tug the pull string.

Speaker grille

Turntable

Voice box casing

Speed regulator

Record

Tone arm

Pull-string Voice Box

Buried inside Woody's body lies the secret to his voice. Operated by a pull string, the voice box comes out with some classic Woody phrases, such as "Reach for the sky!" and "There's a snake in my boot!". However, the hoop of the pull string does have a habit of getting caught on things at the worst possible moments.

Pull-string hoop

Pull string

Despite their shaky start, Buzz and Woody end up being the closest of buddies.

BEST OF FRIENDS?

Sparks fly when Woody and Buzz first meet! Understandably, Buzz is upset about Woody "pushing" him out of Andy's window! However, their friendship is forged in the dangerous world outside Andy's room. The trials and tribulations they face there force them to get along, and show them that they have more in common than they first thought.

Yee-hah!

Even when Woody's arm is torn, the cowboy can't resist helping another toy in despair. But riding off to rescue Wheezy from the yard sale lands Woody in hot water. Al, the unscrupulous Toy Barn owner, "toynaps" the cowboy and locks him away in his penthouse suite. Here, Woody learns that his fate could include a trip to the other side of the world to spend the rest of his life as a museum piece. Are the pull-string cowboy's playing days finally over?

Woody has to choose: life in a museum or playing with Andy?

Woody's once-broken arm

Meet the Gang

Inside Al's apartment, Woody is surprised by some Wild West toys who claim to be from a 1950s TV show. Jessie, a very enthusiastic cowgirl, is thrilled to see him. She takes great delight in showing Woody to the rest of the gang.

BROKEN ARM

During one rough playtime, Andy accidentally breaks the stitching of Woody's arm. As a result, Woody misses out on Cowboy Camp. But when Woody is toynapped, even a broken arm can't stop him from making it back home before Andy returns.

*Shiny cheeks,
airbrushed by
the Cleaner*

*Shoulder joint,
repaired by the
Cleaner*

To Play, or Not to Play

In a curious twist of fate, it's up to Buzz to point out to Woody that his real role is as a toy, not a collectible! Eventually, Woody realizes that even though Andy will grow up, their time together is worth more than anything in the world. After all, a toy's true purpose in life is to make children happy.

*Woody adopts
"playing" state*

Playing Possum

Woody is Andy's favorite toy. Sometimes Andy likes to spin Woody around on the chair or send him flying through the sky to save the day. But while Andy's away and no one is around, Woody and all the toys in Andy's room come to life.

*Boots, freshly shined
by the Cleaner*

BIG IN JAPAN

Al plans to sell the *Woody's Roundup* dolls to a museum in Japan. After initial resistance to the idea, Woody decides to go along to avoid facing the day when Andy will no longer play with him. Al carefully puts the dolls into specially built foam packaging to keep them safe during the long flight to the Konishi Toy Museum in Tokyo.

Buzz Lightyear

When our intergalactic hero bursts onto the scene, the rest of the gang just can't help falling in love with his collection of gadgets. Buzz's mission, however, is to repair his spaceship and leave for the Gamma Quadrant to continue his battle against the evil Emperor Zurg!

Interstellar wing-tip indicator beacon

Buzz has an amazing intellect, as seen when he cracks the code of Al's license plate. Buzz resourcefully chooses the right toys to help him solve the identity of the toynapper.

A Meeting of Minds

The rest of the gang stand open-mouthed in awe when they first meet the gleaming space ranger. Despite Woody's protests that Buzz is seriously deluded, the others are amazed by his multi-phrase voice simulator, laser, and terillium carbonic alloy wings.

BUZZ PROFILE

BUZZ LIGHTYEAR SPACE RANGER

- Buzz Lightyear is a member of the Universe Protection Unit of the Space Ranger Corps.

- He comes from the planet Morph in the Gamma Quadrant of Sector 4, where he protects the galaxy from Zurg.

- Buzz's hobbies include defending the universe, acrobatic stunts, and "falling with style." His favorite saying is "To infinity and beyond!".

_High-pressure,
deep-space visor_

_Multi-phrase voice
simulator_

HERO WORSHIP

Buzz inspires hero worship wherever he goes. Escaping into the rocket-

shaped Space Crane, he is surrounded by aliens who instantly flock to this "stranger from the outside." Buzz then tries to persuade them to take him off this planet and back to his battle with Zurg.

SPACE RANGER LIGHTYEAR

Infrahydraulic wing release activator

_Universe Protection
Unit insignia_

_Terillium
carbonic alloy
wing_

_Intergalactic wrist
communicator_

_Airtight
intergalactic
briefs_

Buzz is brought down to earth when he sees a commercial for himself. The realization that he's a toy, along with the loss of an arm, plunges the space ranger into a pit of despair and causes him to drown his sorrows over a cup of Darjeeling at a doll's tea party.

NO ING TOY.

To Infinity...

Buzz is only saved from his depression when Woody points out to him that, as a toy, he does have a purpose in life—and it's a lot more important than just saving the universe! Instead, he must use all of his hi-tech equipment and gadgetry to keep a little boy happy. Unfortunately, that little boy is about to move to a new home without them!

A disillusioned Buzz sips some Darjeeling at a doll's tea party.

Magnetic radial handgrip

Antigravity servo activator (glows when engaged)

Magnetic radial handgrip

Laser

Buzz's Gear

Every space ranger is equipped with the latest in technology. On his back is a state-of-the-art rocket pack with wings that extend at the touch of a button. The next-generation Buzz comes with a gadget belt. From this, he can pull grappling hooks, engage antigravity servos, and scale walls with his magnetic radials. Buzz also has an intergalactic wrist communicator to keep in touch with Star Command.

Buzz activates his laser using a button on his upper right arm.

Ram air intake

Karate–chop action button

Terillium carbonic alloy wings

Turbojet exhaust ports

The space ranger rocket pack is used for small spacewalks and atmospheric patrols. The terillium carbonic alloy wings spring out at the touch of a button.

SPACESHIP

Buzz's ship is opened by the hands of the eager eight-year-old, Andy. Even though it's damaged, Buzz is trained in every aspect of astromechanics and soon sets to fixing it. Lacking the necessary tools, however, he must improvise using unidirectional bonding strip (sticky tape) and spare parts that he finds around Andy's room.

Taking Charge

Following Woody's "toynapping," Buzz takes charge and briefs the toys on the rescue mission to Al's Toy Barn. All his years of space ranger training have made him ideally suited for such a role—if only the rest of the gang were as well prepared!

Action Hero

When all his gadgets are in full working order, a member of the Universe Protection Unit is able to face nearly any force in the known universe—including children!

Mr. Potato Head

There's only one thing that can tame the acidic wit and dry humor of Mr. Potato Head—and that's his newfound wife, Mrs. Potato Head. She has the ability to turn the cynical root vegetable into mashed potato. However, when she's not around, the other toys better watch out—nobody is safe from his razor-sharp insights!

Mr. Potato Head is upset when he hears that Andy does not get a Mrs. Potato Head for his eighth birthday.

Junior executive model bowler hat

Fashion statement

Toy Chums

Hamm is a match for Mr. Potato Head's wit, and the two quickly become soul mates, playing cards and battleships, telling gags, and talking about the day's proceedings.

Expressive lips for smirking

Gloved hands

Large plastic shoes

Sweet potato lip gloss

POTATO PARTS

The Potato Heads have a whole host of spare parts that can be swapped around to match their various moods, including a pair of angry eyes with eyebrows to match. All of these are kept safely in spare parts compartments, delicately located inside their bodies.

Mrs. Potato Head

She may have the same-shaped body as Mr. Potato Head, but that's where the similarities end. Not only is she far prettier to look at than her husband, she's a lot nicer to know. She's also extremely maternal, and leaps at the chance to adopt three green aliens.

Whenever the mood takes him, Mr. Potato Head uses his detachable body parts to their full effect. He thinks nothing of waving an arm or a leg, a part of his face, or even his eyeballs to get the message across.

Mr. Potato Head has always had a chip on his shoulder about Woody's position as Andy's favorite toy. He's the first toy to point the finger at the pull-string cowboy when Buzz disappears out the bedroom window.

Stylish footwear

POTATO HEAD PROFILE

● In an effort to impress Mrs. Potato Head, Mr. Potato Head rarely wears his mustache when she's around.

● Andy transforms Mr. Potato Head into the outlaw One-Eyed Bart, who rustles sheep and kidnaps the other toys.

● Mr. Potato Head's hobbies include wisecracking, and his favorite phrase is "Yes, my little sweet potato."

Grrrrrrrrrr!

Rex

Even though he's modeled after the most ferocious reptile in history, you couldn't find a more lovable character than Rex. The only danger from Rex is his massive plastic tail. While this hardly sounds dangerous, it's enough to defeat one of the most powerful villains in the universe—Zurg.

Top of the food chain, king of the dinosaurs, but the heart of a leaf-eater!

Plastic, molded dinosaur skin

Zurg whacker

GAME ADDICT

Rex is immediately in awe of Buzz Lightyear. The intrepid space ranger teaches the dizzy dinosaur how to roar properly. The result is unfettered hero worship, to the extent that Rex becomes an avid player of the Buzz Lightyear *Attack on Zurg* Video Game, but has yet to defeat Zurg.

Weak knees

Tyrannosaurus tummy

Sometimes Rex tries to scare the other toys, but the only reaction he gets is mild surprise. By his own admission, Rex has many limitations—he can't even scratch his own nose!

Itty bitty eyes

REX PROFILE

- *Tyrannosaurus rex* evolved during the Cretaceous period and died out some 65 million years ago. Rex was made in 1989 and is still going strong.

- Rex learns how to defeat Zurg from the Video Game Strategy Guide he discovers in Al's Toy Barn. Tips include how to get into Zurg's fortress without being detected!

- Rex's hobbies include playing the Buzz Lightyear *Attack on Zurg* Video Game and working on his roar. His favorite sayings are "I don't like confrontations" and "Did I scare you?".

Toothy grin

360-degree pivoting neck

Tiny arms

THE END

In the end, Rex's clumsiness saves the day. Not wishing to witness the demise of his hero, Rex turns his back on the ugly scene of Zurg defeating Buzz, only to knock the evil one off the elevator and send him plunging to his doom!

Massive clumsy feet

17

Hamm

Hamm is one pig who makes it his business to know everything that's going on—especially if it doesn't concern him. He's also a toy who doesn't like to keep his opinions to himself. And even though he's made from pink plastic, he still thinks he's a cut above the other toys.

Small, piggy ears

Looking Down

Hamm's lofty perch on Andy's shelf means that he looks down on the other toys. He can also see out of Andy's window, and is the first to spot birthday parties and yard sales.

Nosy snout

INSIDES

Lurking inside Hamm is everything an eight-year-old boy saves and can fit through Hamm's slot. These include some coins from around the globe, some pogs, gum wrappers, and a key for Andy's bike lock. All of these can be reached by removing Hamm's cork.

Fast mouth

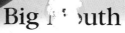

Big Mouth

Hamm's beady eyes and ears pick up any pieces of gossip that go on in Andy's room, which he happily repeats to anyone who will listen.

Coin slot

Plastic body

HAMM PROFILE

- Even though it looks like Hamm's body is made from expensive shiny porcelain, his pink exterior is, in fact, made from cheap, tough, coarse plastic.

- Having lost his original stopper, the hole in Hamm's belly, through which Andy can get at his savings, is now plugged by a wide cork.

- Hamm lists his favorite hobbies as making change and playing battleships and cards with his closest companion, the sharp-witted Mr. Potato Head.

Hamm's cork belly button

Short curly tail

Pig who would be King

In the absence of Woody and Buzz, Hamm is not slow in taking charge of things. His quick wit and fast mouth make sure that he's one piggy bank who's not going to be left on the shelf.

Stumpy leg

He may have a fast mouth, but his legs leave a lot to be desired. Short, stumpy, and with little black nails on the end, Hamm must rely on his quick wit rather than on his physical prowess.

Slinky

As with any dog, Slinky is more than happy to follow the others around, especially Woody. He's also ready to stick his neck out in a tricky situation. His spring means that he can stick it out a lot farther than others, too!

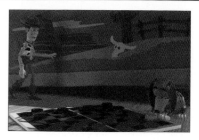

Slinky likes nothing better than a game of checkers with his best pal, Woody.

Even though he takes longer to get around, Slinky always finds himself in the action.

Droopy eyes

Real vinyl floppy ears

Shiny nose

Collar

Rex seeking reassurance

Pull cord attaches here

CANINE COUNSELOR

Slinky may not be the brightest of toys, but his kindly tone and straightforward advice mean that a lot of the other toys turn to him for guidance or reassurance—especially if they have stunted arms and a clumsy tail!

- Slinky represents the comeback of the Slinky toy, which was discontinued in the late 1960s. It took a while for the world to realize that, except for the real thing, a Slinky dog is a kid's best friend.

- Slinky can speak "dog" and acts as a translator between Buster and Woody.

- Slinky is actually equipped with a pair of wheels. These help his hindquarters keep up with the front of his body.

- Slinky's amazing spring can stretch the extendible pooch to over 40 feet (12 meters) in length!

Wheel

Hindquarters

Slinky's hindquarters have a mind of their own. They've even been known to function independently from the front half of his body!

Slinky spring

Spring Power

When there's a rescue needed, or a long drop to bungee, there's only one toy that can step in to do the job. In a dramatic car chase, Slinky's spring is stretched to the limit by Buzz and Woody as they try to catch the moving truck. He also bungees down from the roof of an elevator to try and pull Woody from Al's case as he leaves for the airport.

Foot

Hindquarters

Bo Peep

Even though she's made from porcelain, Bo Peep is far from the delicate type. Not only is she the keeper of her own flock, but she also holds the key to Woody's heart, and can wrap him around her finger. Bo also exudes the calm authority that sets her above Andy's other toys.

Siren Shepherdess

There's only one thing that can melt the heart of Woody—that's the sight of Bo Peep's baby blues. When he's locked under their spell, Woody turns from confident hero into stammering wreck.

Frilly shepherdess dress

Frilly shepherdess bloomers

FAITHFUL FLOCK

Sculptor's shortcut or bizarre genetic nightmare? Whatever you think, Bo's flock behaves much as any flock of sheep does. They follow each other around without thinking, only obey the commands of their shepherd (or shepherdess in this case), and have a tendency to chew their way through anything they can get their teeth on, whether it's remotely edible or not!

New Love?

Even Bo can't fail to be impressed by Buzz's hi-tech gadgets. Could it be that Woody has a rival for his beloved's heart?

Into Action

When the time comes, Bo can turn her big blue eyes to more practical uses. With Lenny's help, she easily spots Buzz and Woody trying to catch up with the moving truck.

The Lady with the Lamp

From her perch beside Molly's bed, Bo can cast her protective gaze over the rest of the room, making sure that nothing is sneaking up to harm her "flock." Bo also uses her crook with a deft hand. With it she can hook her cowboy sweetheart for a quick kiss, or dangle a chain of monkeys out the window.

Removable bonnet

Counting sheep lamp shade

Bo's sheep crook

On/off switch

Lamp stand

Bo Peep's flock

Flower-strewn, porcelain base

BO PEEP PROFILE

• Bo Peep and her flock of sheep belong to Andy's younger sister, Molly. The light Bo provides from her lamp comforts Molly through the night when it gets too dark.

• Bo spends much of her time losing her sheep and then finding them again (usually with Woody's help), and her favorite phrase is one of reassurance to Woody—"Andy will always love you."

Andy's Toys

A ndy's toys are a decidedly mixed bunch, ranging from preschool, educational toys to the latest in intergalactic warriors. Despite this, each of them holds a special place in Andy's heart, as well as a role in the toy society, whether as advance reconnaissance party or comic relief.

With the skill of a crack battalion of troops, the parachutists jump into dangerous territory.

Well-Drilled Unit

The Green Army Men form the toys' eyes and ears in the outside world. Implementing "Recon Plan Charlie," Sarge and his men enter hostile territory to discover what Andy's new presents are. This is one group of men who don't lie down on the job!

TOY PROFILE

- Sarge has a total of 200 plastic troops under his command, each trained and molded for a specific task. Whether there are mines to clear or enemy territory to parachute into, he knows he's got the right men for the job.

- Each of the soldiers is specially trained to march with a plastic base attached to his feet.

- Robot stands on his head and lets Buzz use him as a treadmill to keep the space ranger in peak physical condition.

The evil Dr. Pork Chop (a.k.a. Hamm) commands his minions.

Cowboy Tike

Cap Tike

Sailor Tike

Hunter Tike

Fire Tikes

TALENTED TIKES

They may not say much, but the group of Little Tikes is always on the scene, creating mischief and generally getting in the way. Each Tike sports a different outfit for a different job. These include the artistic Painter Tike and the medical Doc Tike. There are even a few lucky Tikes who get to ride around in their own fire truck, complete with an extendible platform for high-rise high jinks!

little tikes

Shriner Tike

Painter Tike

Doc Tike

Snake and Robot

This enigmatic duo are the engineers of Andy's room. Both of them are chosen by Woody for podium duty, while Robot helps Buzz repair his ship and is an excellent builder with wooden blocks.

Pulsating brain lights

Quizzical snake head

Extendible claw arm

Alphanumeric treads

Flexible snake body

Snake and Robot emerge from under Andy's bed.

Rock Of Gibraltar wrestler's mask

More Toys

In the cozy environment of Andy's room, the toys spend a lot of time in each other's company. They usually all get along with each other and have fun, but inevitably tensions sometimes develop, especially when Buzz disappears out of Andy's window.

Threatening, he-man grimace

Powerful pecs

Bulging biceps

A toy of few words (just the odd grunt), Rocky Gibraltar possesses superhuman strength—well, supertoy strength, that is.

TOY PROFILE

- Rocky is, by far, the strongest toy in Andy's room. He can lift over 50 building blocks!

- Mr. Spell has a vocabulary of nearly 5,000 words—that's nearly 5,000 words more than Rocky Gibraltar!

- Etch A Sketch can draw so quickly that Woody says he has "the fastest knobs in the West!".

Thunderous thighs

Wrestler's boots

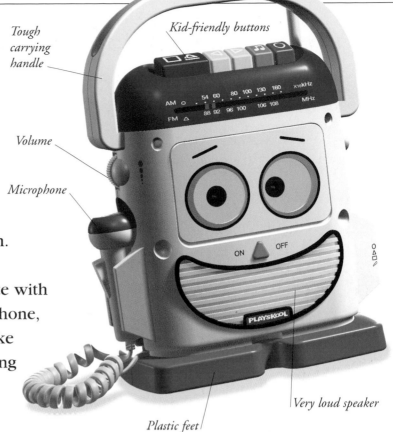

Tough
carrying
handle

Kid-friendly buttons

AM 54 60 80 100 130 160 x10kHz
FM 88 92 96 100 106 108 MHz

Volume

Microphone

ON   OFF

PLAYSKOOL

Very loud speaker

Plastic feet

LOUD MOUTH

Mr. Mike is the loudest toy in Andy's room.
Essentially, he's every kid's first home-
entertainment system. He comes complete with
a cassette player, a radio, and a microphone,
for all those budding junior karaoke
singers. When it comes to talking
over the noise of the others,
he's the only toy for the job!

Mr. Spell

Buzz uses Mr. Spell's mastery of
language to decode the cryptic
license plate on the car that took
Woody. After several tries, they
discover the identity of Woody's
toynapper—Al, the Toy Barn owner.

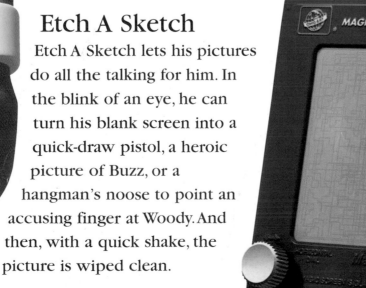

Etch A Sketch

Etch A Sketch lets his pictures
do all the talking for him. In
the blink of an eye, he can
turn his blank screen into a
quick-draw pistol, a heroic
picture of Buzz, or a
hangman's noose to point an
accusing finger at Woody. And
then, with a quick shake, the
picture is wiped clean.

MAGIC *Etch A Sketch* SCREEN

Even More Toys!

There are many toys in Andy's room that prove particularly useful when it comes to an emergency. If you need to see over long distances or cross them very quickly, there's bound to be the right toy for the job waiting somewhere in Andy's toy chest.

Focusing ring

Plastic eyepiece

Long-Lens Lenny

With his long-range vision, Lenny is used to see what's going on in Sid's backyard, and to spot just what Al is up to at the yard sale. However, he's a little slow getting around, and he can take up to 45 minutes to cross Andy's room on his clockwork legs.

RC Car

Need to get somewhere fast? Then you need the RC Car. With a flick of a switch and a turn of the steering wheel, RC Car can zoom across vast distances in the blink of an eye. Naturally, he's the first toy that Woody picks to throw out of the moving truck to rescue Buzz. The following chase, carrying Buzz and Woody, pushes RC Car to the limit—until his batteries run out!

Wheezy

Meet the forgotten toy of the bunch. Andy always played with Wheezy, until one day he squeezed him too hard and his squeaker broke. After that, Wheezy was beset with coughing fits and asthma and was placed on the top shelf to wait for repairs. It all ends happily, as the hapless penguin is rescued from the yard sale by Woody and equipped with a new squeaker.

Wide-angle lens

Magnifying eyes

Wind-up legs

TOY PROFILE

The other toys in Andy's room include:

● Hockey Puck—the mute hockey puck that even has its own arms and legs!

● Troll—with a shock of bright pink hair, the Troll is one toy who stands out in a crowd.

● The Troikas—a collection of hollow dolls, who can hide inside each other at any sign of trouble.

● Andy's ball—used by Buzz as a trampoline!

Andy's ball

Troll

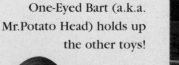

One-Eyed Bart (a.k.a. Mr. Potato Head) holds up the other toys!

Troikas

Andy's House

Inside Andy's room, the toys are free from the dangers of the outside world. However, they are always reminded of how lucky they are; the bedroom window overlooks the neighbor's yard, where less fortunate toys are "taken care of" by Andy's sadistic neighbor, Sid.

Although the toys like playing with children, some children can be too much. Andy's sister tends to drool over anything she gets her hands on!

ANDY PROFILE

- Andy loves his sister, Molly, but moving into his new house means getting his own room.

- Andy has a cowboy hat just like Woody's.

- Andy's favorite restaurant is Pizza Planet, where he enjoys playing the "Black Hole" game.

- Every year, Andy and Woody spend their summer at the Triple R ranch for Cowboy Camp.

Perfect Playroom

Once the door shuts, the toys come out to play. Andy's room makes the perfect playroom, with blue-sky wallpaper and a host of pictures of his favorite toys, especially Woody and Buzz.

Door to outside world

Blue-sky wallpaper

Picture of Andy playing baseball

Amusement park caricatures of Andy and Molly

The other toys watch helplessly as Buzz, Woody, and RC Car try to catch up with the moving truck.

ON THE MOVE

For most of the toys, moving is a well-organized business—they already have their moving buddies to take care of them in transit. Ironically, it's the two heroes, Woody and Buzz, who are left behind, and they must frantically chase the large moving truck as it drives to the new home and Andy's new room.

*Bucket o'
Soldiers*

*ABC
Roundup
poster*

*Cowboy
bedspread*

*Drawings of
Woody by Andy*

Making the Bed

When Woody is Andy's favorite, Andy's bed is covered with cowboy scenes. However, after Andy gets Buzz, Woody is horrified to find that the bed changes in favor of his space ranger toy!

Pizza Planet

Pizza Planet is teeming with screaming kids racing around, filling up on Alien Slime, destroying planets, or lifting small, green aliens into the unknown of the outside world. Buzz and Woody have to plunge into this chaos in order to find their way home to Andy.

Mission Control

Buzz and Woody are faced with a whole host of flashing lights and a bewildering barrage of noise. Over all of this Woody spots Andy and his mom, but Buzz has other ideas and is drawn to the Space Crane.

Gantry

Control room

Spiral staircase

Crew quarters

Planetarium dome

Rocket ship playground

Deep space provisions and pizza

Fuel, oxygen, and soft drink tanks

Guarded Entrance

Pizza Planet is guarded by two gigantic robots. In order to sneak past them, Woody and Buzz must disguise themselves under discarded food cartons.

Deep-dish pepperoni proton rocket motors

Pizza Planet restaurant sign

PIZZA PLANET PROFILE

- Alien Slime comes in any flavor you want—as long as it's green!

- Other video games at Pizza Planet include Combat Wombat, Hurl, Kabookey, Planet Killer, Whack-A-Alien, and Scooter Patrol.

Kabookey!

THE CLAW

Inside the Space Crane, Woody and Buzz are swamped by short, three-eyed aliens. Before long, however, the all-powerful claw is plucking the chosen ones out from the crowd for life in the outside world. Unfortunately, the person controlling the claw happens to be Sid, the evil toy torturer, and Buzz and Woody are in danger!

Dodging through the crowds of screaming children, Woody follows Buzz into the Space Crane game.

Mission control

Planet Killer

Whack-A-Alien

Space Crane game

Diner booths

Alien Slime

Video games

Robot guarded airlock entrance

Pizza Planet Delivery Shuttles carry their pizza cargo to the neighborhood (serving your local star cluster).

Sid's House

Janie Doll waiting to undergo surgery

Welcome to the twisted, dark world of Sid's house. Within its eerie walls, toys are forced to undergo radical surgery to create hideous mutants. Worse still, when Buzz arrives, he is dressed in a frilly apron and forced to have a cup of Darjeeling with Hannah's dolls!

Single, unshaded light bulb

Sid's room is filled with various kinds of toy torturing equipment.

Sid's toolbox

SID PROFILE

• While playing the Space Crane at Pizza Planet, Sid is pleasantly surprised to grab not only a Buzz Lightyear, but also a cowboy doll—both with the same quarter!

• Sid's favorite tool of toy torture is the magnifying glass. With it, he focuses the sun's light onto a toy to create a burning ray!

• Sid faces a $500 fine for the illegal possession of the upturned milk crate on his desk.

Sid, the evil toy torturer

Sid's house is next door to Andy's, and Woody manages to throw a string of Christmas lights between them to try and get back to his owner.

The Backyard

Sid's backyard is a burial ground for toys. Many abused toys lie buried in the mud, only to rise up in the final showdown to scare Sid to his senses.

Paul Bunyan poster

Sid's shelves are filled with the gruesome trophies of his cruelty. The lava lamp contains the severed heads of toys, trapped forever to float in the clear liquid.

Doll-filled lava lamp

Illegally obtained milk crate

SCUD MISSILE

Patrolling the corridors of Sid's house is the streak of canine lightning that is Scud. With an impressive array of toy-chewing teeth in his jaws, Scud is one dog that Woody and Buzz want to avoid. This is a lot harder than it sounds, as Scud is always alert for things to destroy. It takes a lot of precise planning, some eye-popping stunts, and an immense amount of toy heroics to outwit the hair-raising hound.

Scud is always alert for toys to chew.

The Mutant Toys

Locked in the dark and sinister world of Sid's room lie the creations of his warped and sick imagination. Over the years, Sid has put together a nightmarish collection of mutant toys by mutilating bits and pieces of toys that fall into his clutches.

Returning from Pizza Planet inside Sid's bag, Woody is horrified at what he might find inside Sid's room.

Spider baby

Babyhead is a hideous-looking cross between the head of a baby doll and a construction set. Despite having less-than-delicate-looking claws, it reconnects Buzz's arm with the skill of a surgeon.

MUTANT TOY PROFILE

• When they first see the mutant toys, Buzz and Woody believe that they are cannibals, as the mutants flock around the dissected remains of Pterodactyl and Janie Doll.

• The toys use the extendible hand of Hand-in-the-box to open the door of Sid's room, letting out the Frog and luring Scud away.

• Babyhead used to belong to Hannah. But Hannah hasn't seen her doll for a long time now, as Babyhead lurks under Sid's bed to escape from its evil tormentor.

• While Woody distracts Sid from lighting the rocket, the other mutants sneak around Sid's yard "waking up" some of the toys that Sid has blown up.

Legs

Roller Bob

Ducky

Frog

Rockmobile

Babyhead

Jingle Joe

Mutant Car

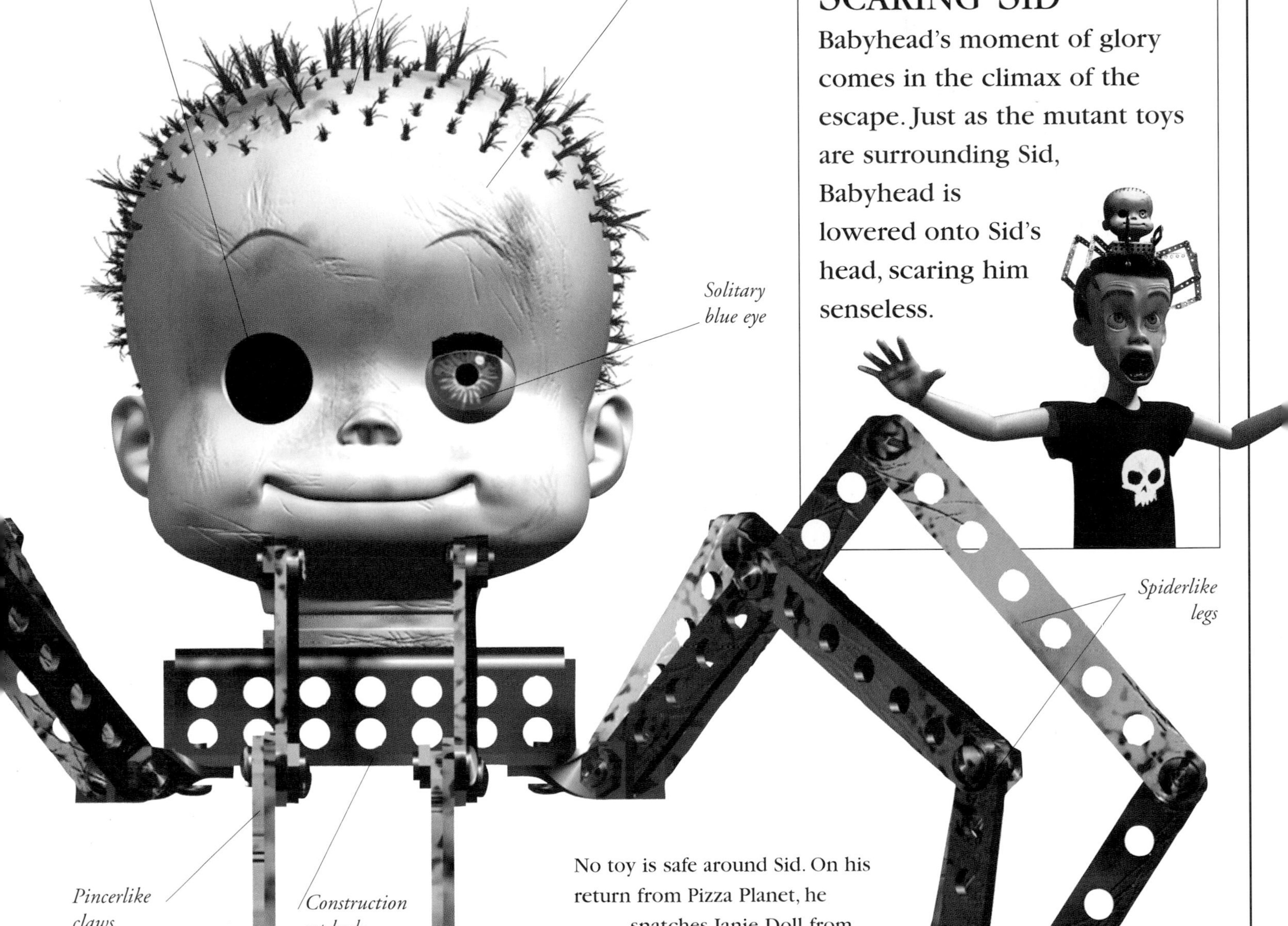

Missing eye

Stubbly hair

Baby doll's head

Solitary blue eye

Babyhead's moment of glory comes in the climax of the escape. Just as the mutant toys are surrounding Sid, Babyhead is lowered onto Sid's head, scaring him senseless.

Spiderlike legs

Pincerlike claws

Construction set body

No toy is safe around Sid. On his return from Pizza Planet, he snatches Janie Doll from the hands of Hannah and rushes upstairs to perform an impromptu head transplant.

Even with only one and a half wheels, Frog is still the fastest toy in Sid's house.

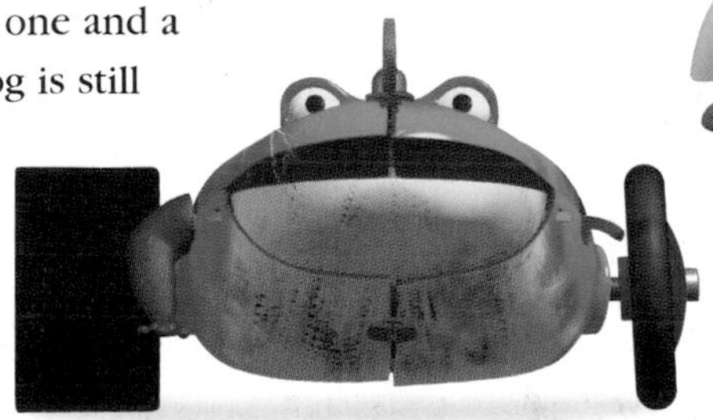

Wind the Frog

With his speed, Frog is the only toy fast enough to distract Scud. The start of Buzz and Woody's escape from Sid's house is heralded by Mutant Car winding Frog's clockwork key.

More Mutants

Even though Sid's creations appear hideous and scary at first, they do not hesitate to come to the aid of Woody and Buzz. Their action-packed heroics distract Scud and frighten Sid, allowing Woody and Buzz to escape from Sid's house, thereby setting up the epic chase that gets them back to Andy.

Pterodactyl

Pterodactyl is the unfortunate doll who has its head transplanted onto Janie Doll. Happily, the other mutants swap the heads back, and Pterodactyl can see the world with its own eyes.

Fishing hook

Ducky and Legs

Steadied by the shapeliest pair of legs you'll see in a toy chest, Legs uses her fishing rod to lower Ducky through the light hole in the porch. From here, the duck's head stuck on a baby's body swings to ring the doorbell and then drops down to pluck Frog from the jaws of Scud.

Doll's legs

Ducky head

Doll's body

Spring

Hand-in-the-box

Roller Bob

Rockmobile

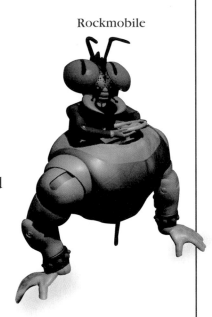

Healthy Imagination?

The mutants are the result of Sid's imagination. Hand-in-the-box has a severed hand in place of Jack. Roller Bob has the body of a pilot screwed to a skateboard, while Rockmobile has an insect's head stuck onto a Combat Carl torso, which is stuck onto a Rocky Gibraltar body!

Jingle Bells

Jingle Joe isn't a toy that can stay quiet for long—in fact, he can't stay quiet at all! His jingling roller means you can hear him long before you see him. On top of this is a Combat Carl head, while a toy arm makes sure that Joe stays upright at all times.

The escape is planned out in incredible detail, with Woody, as ever, organizing every step.

ESCAPE!

Once launch day arrives and Sid takes Buzz outside, Woody leaps into action and starts to plan an escape and rescue mission. This involves Frog distracting the sharp-toothed Scud, and the other toys making a dash for the backyard through the dog door. Once there, the toys proceed to break the rules a little and "come alive" in front of Sid, surrounding the toy torturer and scaring him out of his mind!

Woody scaring Sid

The Neighborhood

The toys' many adventures all take place in the Tri-County area. Scattered throughout this district are both of Andy's homes, Pizza Planet, the Dinoco Gas Station, and Al's Toy Barn and apartment. On the outskirts is the Tri-County Airport, where the final breathtaking rescue takes place.

The toys re-create the neighborhood in miniature in Andy's room.

Nightmare Neighbor

Sid's house lies next door to Andy's first home—so close, in fact, that Andy's toys can shout across to Woody when he's held hostage in Sid's bedroom.

New Home

Andy's new home is in a much nicer part of the Tri-County area. Basically, anywhere away from Sid is a nicer part of town to live in, especially when you're a toy!

Sid's rocket

On the Road

All seems lost for Buzz and Woody when the batteries in RC Car run out. That is, until Woody has the bright idea of lighting the rocket. In the blink of an eye, the three toys are zooming through the air, covering the yards between them and the moving truck and Andy. The only problem is, what happens when the rocket goes boom?

HIGH-RISE RESCUE!

Al's luxury penthouse sits on top of a twenty-three-floor apartment building, just across the road from Al's Toy Barn. To reach Woody, the toy rescue team has to climb up the building's elevator shaft, with the evil Emperor Zurg in pursuit.

Al's apartment building

Toy Barn

Just 20 blocks from Andy's house lies Al's Toy Barn. While only a short bike ride for us humans, it takes Buzz and his toy rescue party all night to cross what for them is a huge distance. When they get there, they still have to cross a busy and extremely dangerous street.

Pizza Planet

Formerly the site of "Chateau d'If," the cordon bleu French restaurant which burned to the ground several years ago, Pizza Planet now offers totally different fare. Deep-pan pizzas and Alien Slime are dispatched to hordes of screaming kids.

Dinoco

The Dinoco gas station offers a rest spot between Andy's house and Pizza Planet. It's also where the bickering Buzz and Woody manage to lose Andy and get stranded on the forecourt of the gas station.

Al's World

Meet the shiftiest toy store owner there is. This man would sell his own limited edition chicken watch to get the doll of his dreams—Woody. Al McWhiggin is so driven to complete his *Woody's Roundup* collection that he resorts to thievery. Little does he realize that hot on his trail is a band of toys whose mission is to rescue the cowboy and bring him back to Andy's room.

Vintage eye glasses

Oily complexion

The grand entrance to Al's apartment building is just across the street from the Toy Barn.

AL'S PROFILE

● As a child, Al quit playing with toys when he discovered he could make money selling them. This explains why he feels no qualms about stealing and selling other children's toys!

● Al's hobbies include collecting toys (not to play with!), and eating cheese puffs.

Baggy, short-legged trousers

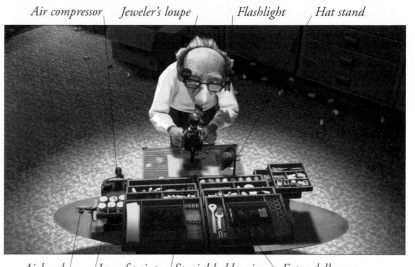

Air compressor   *Jeweler's loupe*   *Flashlight*   *Hat stand*

Airbrush   *Jars of paints*   *Special hobby vice*   *Extra doll arms*

Going Up

The elevator in Al's apartment building is the scene of Slinky's heroic attempt to rescue Woody. Meanwhile, on the elevator roof, Buzz, Deluded Buzz, and Rex do battle with Zurg.

Toy Barn chicken watch

In the Office

Al faxes details of the *Woody's Roundup* toys through to his Japanese clients. While he's on the phone, Buzz and the rest of the rescue party sneak into his bag.

Al's car carries the license plate that tells the toys where Woody has been taken.

Gas Guzzler

Al's car is a 1958 Acorn he's had for 30 years. There are few left in the world and they are highly collectible, as are most things belonging to Al.

Woody's Roundup

Running for just one season in 1957, *Woody's Roundup* was, for a short time at least, the number-one children's television show. In Al's apartment, Woody comes face-to-face with his past, not only as part of a set of western toys, but also as the high-ridin'est, rootin'-tootin'est TV hero of all time.

Woody stares, open-mouthed in disbelief, at his own TV show.

Marionettes

Unlike the lively toys that Woody, Bullseye, and Jessie are in real life, the characters on the TV show were played by marionettes—puppets controlled by strings. These puppets would enact the week's drama in front of a cardboard set.

A selection of stills from the TV series

ROUNDUP TIME

A typical episode of *Woody's Roundup* begins with Jessie and the Prospector going down into an old mine in search of a legendary giant gold nugget. However, the Prospector accidentally causes the mine entrance to collapse; and then, in his panic, he lights the fuse to a dynamite keg instead of a candle! Jessie then yodels for her critters, who fetch Sheriff Woody to save the day.

Western Buddies

Woody is stunned to meet the other toys from the *Woody's Roundup* series. The other characters are Bullseye, the sharpest horse in the West, Jessie, the yodeling cowgirl, and Stinky Pete, the Prospector. However, Woody's joy is short-lived when he learns that the set of toys has been sold and is due to be shipped to a museum in Japan!

ROUNDUP PROFILE

● A total of 13 episodes of *Woody's Roundup* were made. All of these episodes were brought to you by Cowboy Crunchies, "the only cereal that's sugar-frosted and dipped in chocolate."

● *Woody's Roundup* was popular from the start. Even though it only ran for one season, millions of fans tuned in each week to watch Woody's on-screen adventures.

● The show was finally pulled after the launch of Sputnik in 1957, when kids' interests switched from the Wild West to outer space!

Jessie, the cowgirl

Stinky Pete, the Prospector

Bullseye

Woody chases Jessie

Bullseye galloping happily

Jessie enjoys playing again

Record player arm

Woody's Roundup theme song

Woody and Bullseye

Together, Woody and Bullseye form a team that aims to bring the law back to the West—and to entertain the viewers with a few songs from Woody's guitar. Their adventures take them through some hair-raising scrapes and near misses, but none quite so hair-raising as rescuing Jessie from a jetliner as it accelerates down the runway.

Friendly wave

Jessie, Woody, and Bullseye prepare for a quick getaway.

Unhappy Horse

Bullseye is very upset when the cowboy refuses to join the other *Woody's Roundup* toys and go to Japan. He soon perks up, however, when he learns that he'll play with Andy and not be locked up in a museum.

CELEBRITY

Despite its short run, *Woody's Roundup* was extremely popular. Woody and the gang's fame on the show inspired the creation of several games and books. There was a set of *Woody's Roundup* playing cards, a book of guitar songs, and "Pin the Tail on Bullseye" was a favorite at children's birthday parties.

LEARN GUITAR WITH WOODY

WOODY TEACHES YOU HIS FAVORITE SONGS: CHUCK WAGON BRAGGIN', COWBOY BLUES, ACCORDION TO ME, AND MANY MORE.

"LEARN MY FAVORITE SONGS"

8 EASY TO LEARN GUITAR TECHNIQUES

FREE ROUNDUP PICK INSIDE.

Woody's CARD GAME

Woody's ROUNDUP

QUICK ON THE DRAW

AGES 6 & UP

Made in Point Richmond USA

COMIC-BOOK HERO

During its period on television, *Woody's Roundup* ran alongside a spin-off weekly comic book. In these, our hero Woody, with the help of his constant companion Bullseye, would outsmart rustlers and rescue animals in distress. The comic books managed to outlive the TV series by a year, before children turned their attention to other heroes.

Ears alert and ready for action

Rustler-sniffing nose

Grinning teeth

Stirrup

Floppy legs

Bullseye is known as "the sharpest horse in the West" because of his keen senses of smell and sight. Thanks to these, no bandit could escape from Sheriff Woody.

BULLSEYE PROFILE

• Bullseye's hide is made from a soft but sturdy, double-stitched brown corduroy—built to withstand the hardships of a long day on the ranch.

• Bullseye is an expert horseshoe thrower. He earned his name by tossing 17 ringers in a row during a game of horseshoes—he even used his own shoes!

• Bullseye's hobby is riding the range. He has no favorite sayings or phrases, relying instead on a number of happy-sounding horse noises to let others know how he feels.

Jessie

As Woody's sidekick, Jessie's the sassiest, brassiest cowgirl you could ever meet. In her hand-sewn hat and fake cowhide chaps, she can lasso a stray critter at 60 paces and certainly knows how to take care of herself. However, her confident exterior hides a more tragic past.

Jessie has her own merchandise, including a "Critter Call" record.

Ten-pint cowgirl hat

Yarn hair

Rosy cheeks

Cowgirl pony tail

Crazy Critters

Whenever Jessie yodels, a whole host of animals come to her aid. These crazy critters include snakes, armadillos, flying squirrels, buck-toothed bears, and beavers.

Roundup Ranch belt buckle

Fringed shirt

Hard-wearing cowgirl jeans

Fake cowhide chaps

JESSIE PROFILE

- Jessie the doll was once owned by a little girl named Emily. But Emily grew up and gave Jessie away.

- Jessie now has a fear of being abandoned. When Woody says that he's leaving, she breaks down, fearing a life in the darkness of storage.

- Jessie's hobbies include yodeling and playing with her critters. Her favorite phrase is "Yee-hah!".

Jessie even has a lunchbox with her picture on it!

Cowgirl boots

Prospector

Prospector's TV character, Stinky Pete, bungles his way through the *Woody's Roundup* series, letting Woody rescue him from a variety of scrapes. However, the real Prospector hides a far more selfish character!

The Prospector's innocent-looking TV character

Mint Condition

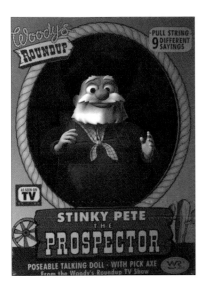

Never a popular toy, Stinky Pete the Prospector languished on a dime-store shelf for many years before being discovered by Al, the Toy Barn owner. Even today, he never steps outside his box, employing Bullseye to move him around.

Floppy prospector's hat

Innocent-looking features

Fake gold tooth

Large prospector's belly

PROSPECTOR PROFILE

• The Prospector is mighty handy with his pick, using it to screw the ventilation grille shut and stop the toys from escaping.

• His hobbies include keeping himself in mint condition, and his favorite saying is "It's a dangerous world out there for a toy."

• Stinky Pete, the TV character, got his name because he only took a bath once a month.

Prospector's pick

Collect Them All!

Even though just 13 episodes of *Woody's Roundup* were made, an incredible amount of show-related merchandise was snatched off the shelves by enthusiastic fans. The show's early demise simply added to the value of these items, which include everything from bubble pumps to lunchboxes.

It's Woody Time

Woody's arms point to the correct time, while the bells on this alarm clock made sure that kids would get out of bed on time and never miss an episode of their favorite western show.

Bullseye mug

Cowboy boot lamp *Autographed picture of Woody* *Wall clock*

Woody's Roundup radio *Lunchbox*

Bubbles Anyone?

This bubble pump in the shape of Woody's face lets you blow dozens of soap bubbles simply by pushing down his hat!

Money in the Bank

Simply place a coin on the Prospector's gold pan and watch as he flips it over his head to Woody, who drops it in the "orphans' fund." This encouraged kids to save—and have fun at the same time!

COLLECTIBLE PROFILE

- The complete set of Woody's Roundup dolls fetches Al a hefty sum. It would have been worth a lot more, but Woody didn't come with his original box.

- Some merchandising ideas never got off the drawing board. These include Bullseye's Glue, Stinky Pete Eau de Cologne, Woody's Cattle Branding kit, and Jessie's Critter Cages.

Chow pan

Al's Treasure

One room in Al's penthouse suite is filled with memorabilia and collectibles from the *Woody's Roundup* series. Al has made it his personal mission to collect anything to do with the 1950s show—and now that he has Woody, he's got the whole set!

Woody's Roundup comics

Set for cardboard theater

Prospector character for cardboard theater

Record player | *Woody character for cardboard theater*

Thirsty Work

The *Woody's Roundup* thermos bottle and lunchbox made sure that a cowboy's lunch was kept fresh to eat out on the ranch. They were also made from tough tin to take the knocks of a day in the saddle!

Thermos bottle and lunchbox— vital for the hungry cowboy.

Al's Toy Barn

Sitting on the corner of Cutting and Canal streets is Al's Toy Barn, the giant toy emporium famous for selling the best toys at cheap, cheap, cheap prices! Al built this, his first store, before constructing several Toy Barn outlets across the Tri-County area. Since then, these fake farmyard stores have spread throughout the country.

The toys enter the mysterious world of the closed Toy Barn.

Realistic-looking tiled roof

Toy-packed aisles

Al's Toy Barn sign

Realistic-looking tin roof

Al's Bucks

Al puts on his chicken suit when he appears in Toy Barn TV commercials. He promotes the latest bargains that will save the customer "Buck, buck, bucks!"

Entrance pressure pad

Checkout counters

Shopping cart

DOWN ON THE FARM

Al carried the farm theme throughout the entire toy store. The shopping carts are designed to look like cows and even the main buildings resemble a huge barn and grain silo. But it is just a thin facade. Directly behind the cute-looking barn sits an enormous and extremely ugly warehouse where the toys are stored.

Grain silo

Realistic-looking, fake barn

Cow jumping over the moon

Miles of Aisles

The inside of Al's Toy Barn is filled with aisle after aisle of toys that stretch from the floor to the ceiling. Each shelf is crammed to bursting with a whole host of exciting toys. These include the next-generation Buzz Lightyear, complete with utility belt.

Giant chicken stands guard in front of Al's Toy Barn, unveiled today in a gala ceremony.

Big New Toy Store Opens– Barn Theme a Hit with Kiddies

By Geoff Brannon

A giant new toy emporium, Al's Toy Barn, dubbed by the owner as "Grandest in the Tri-County area", opened today with as much hoopla and fanfare as could be mustered given the threatening skies and chill breeze.

Owner Al McWhiggin was on hand for the festivities, which began with Sousa marches played by the Warren G. Harding High School band and culminated with the release of 100 feral rock doves symbolizing, as Mr. McWhiggin put it "The spirit of the common man, free and unfettered by unfair taxation!" (McWhiggin has been campaigning unsuccessfully for two years to repeal a 125 year old state tax on wealthy landowners in the area. The tax was originally designed as an attempt to curtail rampant unchecked profiteering by such greedy land barons as McWhiggin's Great Grandfather, Horace P. McWhiggin, one of the founders of the "Real Americans"

for Manifest Destiny", a 19th century men's club promoting rampant unchecked profiteering and the relocation of the Tri-County's once thriving Indian tribe, the gentle Wannapeesanee.)

The building is a cinderblock structure designed to mimic the look of a traditional country barn from days gone by. There is a three story silo featuring the Cow who jumped over the moon from Mother Goose tales. The little ones seemed more thrilled than the irascible McWhiggin who, as he cut the ceremonial ribbon to open the doors, was visibly uncomfortable in the presence of so many fresh faced and eager tots.

Al's Toy Barn is situated on the corner of Cutting and Canal Streets on the site of the old Veteran's Charity Hospital, which was razed two years ago to make way for this new retail structure. The big toy store has as it's main landmark a 20-foot tall sculpture of a crudely formed chicken on a concrete base.

OPENING DAY

Al McWhiggin opened the first Al's Toy Barn in the Tri-County area in October 1963. The event was accompanied by a marching band from the local school and the release of 100 feral rock doves.

The highlight of the festivities was the unveiling of the enormous 20 foot (6 meter) high sculpture of an egg-shaped chicken. This huge statue still stands at the entrance to the massive toy store.

Zurg

Pathetic mortals, behold the awesome figure of the evil Emperor Zurg! He is called the Scourge of the Gamma Quadrant and the Sworn Destroyer of the Galactic Alliance, and is the arch nemesis of the space ranger Buzz Lightyear. His sole aim is to crush the puny space ranger and continue his mission to conquer the universe.

Targeting sight

Zurgotronic ion blaster

Free to Wreak Havoc

Zurg is freed from his hypersleep when Buzz inadvertently pushes a pile of boxes over to open the Toy Barn doors. Unfortunately, Zurg's is one of them. As the doors close, they force open Zurg's box lid, releasing the emperor!

ZURG PROFILE

• Zurg hails from the planet Xrghthung, a nasty place that is as evil as it is unpronounceable.

• Obsessed by his own image, Zurg has built the entrance to his evil fortress in the shape of his initial—a gigantic "Z."

• Even though Buzz's space ranger suit is made from a rare terillium carbonic alloy (one of the toughest compounds in the known universe), it is still vulnerable to the power of Zurg's ion blaster.

EVIL EMPEROR
Zurg
ARCH ENEMY OF
BUZZ LIGHTYEAR
Made in USA

Awe-inspiring imperial stance

Imperial Cloak
of Deception

Evil,
glowing
eyes

Threatening
Horns of
Neptar

Vile,
yellow
teeth

Zurg's Imperial
medallion

Emperor's
official battle
armor

Evil-looking,
clawlike hand

Ammo Pack

Zurg carries his ion pellets in
his backpack. With each pull
of the trigger, a pellet flies
along the delivery tube
and out one of the
blaster's three barrels.

Ammo
delivery
tube

Power level
indicator

BUZZ DESTROYER

Zurg's main weapon of choice is his
Zurgotronic ion blaster. When primed and
ready, this evil weapon dispatches ion bolts
with deadly accuracy. Its power level
indicator even goes up to "11"—for extra
Buzz-destroying power!

A Dorling Kindersley Book

SENIOR ART EDITOR John Kelly

PROJECT EDITOR Jon Richards

PROJECT ART EDITOR Robert Perry

DESIGNERS Kim Browne & Guy Harvey

MANAGING EDITOR Joanna Devereux

MANAGING ART EDITOR Cathy Tincknell

US EDITOR Gary Werner

DTP DESIGNER Jill Bunyan

PRODUCTION Steve Lang & Jo Rooke

ADDITIONAL ART Ed Danté

Published in the United States by
Dorling Kindersley Publishing, Inc., 95 Madison Avenue, New York, New York 10016
First American Edition, 1999
2 4 6 8 10 9 7 5 3 1

A catalog record is available from the Library of Congress.
ISBN 0-7894-5312-6

Dorling Kindersley books are available at special discounts for bulk purchases for sales promotions or premiums. Special editions, including personalized covers, excerpts of existing guides, and corporate imprints can be created in large quantities for specific needs. For more information, contact Special Markets Dept./Dorling Kindersley Publishing, Inc./95 Madison Ave./New York, NY 10016/Fax: 800-600-9098.

Reproduced by Media Development, England
Printed and bound by World Color, USA

Acknowledgments

Mr. Potato Head® and Mrs. Potato Head® are registered trademarks of Hasbro, Inc.

Used with permission. © Hasbro Inc. All rights reserved;

Slinky® Dog © James Industries;

Etch A Sketch® © The Ohio Art Company;

Toddle Tots® by Little Tikes® and Fire Truck by Little Tikes®

Little Tikes Toys © The Little Tikes Company;

© Lego Systems, Inc.

Troll Doll © Russ Berrie and Company

Dorling Kindersley would like to thank:

Leeann Alameda, John Lasseter, Ash Brannon, Lee Unkrich, Helene Plotkin, Karen Robert Jackson, Katherine Sarafian, Kathleen Handy, Clay Welch, David Haumann, Jim Pearson, Dan Jeup, Ralph Eggleston, Bob Pauley, Bill Cone, Jonas Rivera, Alethea Harampolis, Edward Chen, and the staff at Pixar Animation Studios; Hunter Heller, Eric Huang, Victoria Saxon, and Tim Lewis at Disney Publishing; Mike Vollaro at Speak-Up!, Shirley, NY 11967, USA.